DESIGNING
Positive
School
Communities

Design Thinking

for a Better World

Janice Dyer

CRABTREE
PUBLISHING COMPANY
WWW.CRABTREEBOOKS.COM

Author: Janice Dyer

Series research and development:
Reagan Miller and Janine Deschenes

Editors: Janine Deschenes and Margaret McClintock

Editorial director: Kathy Middleton

Editorial services: Clarity Content Services

Proofreader: Angela Kaelberer

Production coordinator and prepress technician:
Tammy McGarr

Print coordinator: Katherine Berti

Cover design: Tammy McGarr

Design: David Montle

Photo Research: Linda Tanaka

Credits:
p4 antoniodiaz/shutterstock; p6 Jacob Lund/Fotolia; p7 rawpixel/shutterstock; p8 Rawpixel/shutterstock; p9 Photo courtesy of Rymfire. Photo originally appeared in the Palm Coast Observer; p11 Rawpixel/shutterstock; p12 SkyLinks/shutterstock; pp12-13 Ellagrin/shutterstock; p14 ronstik/dreamstime; p15 top Pumikan Sawatroj/dreamstime, Dean Drobot/shutterstock; pp16-17 sek_suwat/shutterstock; p18 Chinnapong/shutterstock; p19 29september/shutterstock; p20 stock_photo_world/shutterstock; p21 A_stockphoto/shutterstock; p22 DGLimages/shutterstock; p23 Stephen Barnes/Bowline Images/Alamy/All Canada Photos; p24 Ehab Othman/shutterstock; p25 ravipat/shutterstock; p26 Monkey Business Images/shutterstock; p27 Jacob Lund/Fotolia; p28 MediaPictures.pl/shutterstock; p29 eamesbot/shutterstock; p30 Meghan Mccarthy/The Palm Beach Post via ZUMA Wire/Alamy/All Canada Photos; p31 Mandy Godbehear/shutterstock; p33 YAY Media AS/Alamy/All Canada Photos; p34 RosaIreneBetancourt 12/Alamy/All Canada Photos; p35 Jacob Lund/Fotolia; p36 Mandy Godbehear/shutterstock; p37 Photo courtesy of Jaylens Challenge Foundation, Inc.; p38 Mandy Godbehear/shutterstock; p39 SpeedKingZ/shutterstock; p40 tommaso79/shutterstock; p41 Syda Productions/shutterstock; p42 Frances Roberts/Alamy/All Canada Photos; p43 Jacob Lund/Fotolia; p44 Monkey Business Images/shutterstock.

Library and Archives Canada Cataloguing in Publication

Dyer, Janice, author
    Designing positive school communities / Janice Dyer.

(Design thinking for a better world)
Includes bibliographical references and index.
Issued in print and electronic formats.
ISBN 978-0-7787-4462-7 (hardcover).--
ISBN 978-0-7787-4541-9 (softcover).--
ISBN 978-1-4271-2037-3 (HTML)

    1. School environment--Juvenile literature. 2. Classroom environment--Juvenile literature. I. Title.

LC210.D94 2018   j371.102'4   C2017-908092-X
                                      C2017-908093-8

Library of Congress Cataloging-in-Publication Data

Names: Dyer, Janice, author.
Title: Designing positive school communities / Janice Dyer.
Description: New York, New York : Crabtree Publishing Company, [2018] | Series: Design thinking for a better world | Includes bibliographical references and index.
Identifiers: LCCN 2017060373 (print) | LCCN 2018011639 (ebook) | ISBN 9781427120373 (Electronic) | ISBN 9780778744627 (hardcover) | ISBN 9780778745419 (pbk.).
Subjects: LCSH: Community and school--Juvenile literature. | Problem solving--Juvenile literature.
Classification: LCC LC215 (ebook) | LCC LC215 .D93 2018 (print) | DDC 371.19--dc23
LC record available at https://lccn.loc.gov/2017060373

Crabtree Publishing Company

www.crabtreebooks.com   1-800-387-7650

Printed in the U.S.A./052018/CG20180309

Published in Canada
Crabtree Publishing
616 Welland Ave.
St. Catharines, Ontario
L2M 5V6

Published in the United States
Crabtree Publishing
PMB 59051
350 Fifth Avenue, 59th Floor
New York, New York 10118

Published in the United Kingdom
Crabtree Publishing
Maritime House
Basin Road North, Hove
BN41 1WR

Published in Australia
Crabtree Publishing
3 Charles Street
Coburg North
VIC, 3058

Contents

hen you see a problem in the world around you, do you want to help solve it? If so, then design thinking may be for you.

Design thinking is a **process**—a set of steps to take you to your goal. It's also a **mindset**—a set of attitudes a person has about something. You can use design thinking to look at problems in a new way and find brilliant solutions. Design thinking is a powerful, people-focused way to help people of all ages and backgrounds become **change makers** in their communities.

The Focus: People's Needs

Design thinkers start with **empathy** for the user, or the person or group who is experiencing a problem. They work to understand the problem from the **user's** point of view. Design thinkers stay focused on the user and the user's needs as they work to develop a solution.

Working with a partner or a small group will help you come up with new ideas while working through the design-thinking process.

Where Did Design Thinking Come From?

User-focused problem solving is an approach that has been used for years, under many different names. Design thinking is also called public-interest design, because it is a way to inspire people to work together to create solutions that are in the interest, or will benefit, people in a **community**. You can use design thinking to help you find solutions to all kinds of problems.

Meet a
CHANGE
MAKER

Jeremiah Anthony
Taking Action against Cyberbullies

Jeremiah Anthony was a student at West High School in Iowa City, Iowa, when he learned about cyberbullying. Cyberbullies target others on social media, usually writing hurtful messages and posting them publicly or sending them privately. Many teens use social media sites daily. Jeremiah learned that some students at his school were being cyberbullied. They felt bad about themselves every time they used social media. He listened to their experiences and decided to make social media a positive place for them.

> "When I got the tweet it just really brightened up my day that someone would send a tweet like that."

Jeremiah created a Twitter account, @westhighbros, to tweet compliments to students he thought might be feeling bad that day. His friends started tweeting compliments to their friends, who then tweeted their friends. Thousands of tweets later, sending sincere compliments to other students has become a regular part of life at Jeremiah's school. Jeremiah and his friends were inspired to make a difference in their school and community by reminding people of their value and strengths.

> "What he is doing with complimenting people, one compliment can change their entire life."

Jeremiah Anthony explains: "Cyberbullies try to focus on what's bad about a person, and I try to say, no, you're actually really good at this, and you're much more good at this than you're bad at this."

---

westhighbros @westhighbros

You are so full of character and energy. You're a great friend to anyone and can find the good in everything.

💬 3   🔁 2   🤍 2

The Design-thinking Process

The design-thinking process is a set of steps that guides problem solving. There are a few different versions of the process, but all of them focus on putting the user's needs first.

Loop the Loop

The design-thinking process we will use in this book has six steps. Often, you won't find the solution to a problem on your first try.

1. Empathize
Develop a deep understanding of the user's needs.

2. Define
Identify a point of view and define a problem to solve.

3. Ideate
Generate many creative ideas as possible solutions.

4. Prototype
Build a representation or model of the best idea.

5. Test
Share prototype with user and get feedback.

6. Reflect
Evaluate how well the solution met the user's needs.

Design thinking is an iterative process. This means you can repeat the steps many times as you work toward a solution.

Members of positive school communities **respect** each other's ideas and needs.

Design thinkers don't give up if their first ideas don't work. Design thinkers **fail forward**, meaning they use mistakes and failures to improve their solution on the next try.

Community Connections

A community can be small, such as your class at school, or large, such as a whole country.

Have you heard the expression "Think globally, act locally"? It means we help the whole planet when we make positive change in our own small part of the world.

Positive school communities make everyone feel welcome, safe, and included. You can use design thinking to help create positive school communities at your school and around the world. This book shows you how.

Mindset Tips

Be interested	Listen to other people. Learn about their lives.
Dig deep	Be curious. Explore. Ask lots of questions.
Share	Work on problems with others. Value their ideas.
Be open	New ideas can come from unexpected places.
Be brave	Try out original ideas. Don't let fear of failing stop you.

Empathize

What Is Empathy?

Empathy is the ability to understand the feelings of others. Design thinkers use empathy to help them see a problem through the eyes of the person experiencing the problem.

To spend time with a user in your school community, you could ask to sit together at lunch or be partners in a classroom activity or field trip.

Empathy allows design thinkers to identify the needs of the person or people experiencing a problem. A need is any requirement that a person or group has. A person's needs are specific to them. They can be physical, social, and **cultural**.

In a school community, a physical need could be a safe area for students to voice their concerns or a space that students with physical **disabilities** can access. A cultural need could be allowing students time to practice their cultural or religious traditions. A social need could be ensuring that all students are able to participate in extracurricular activities.

Learning How to Empathize

The best way to understand a person's thoughts, feelings, and needs is to spend time with them. Ask questions about their life. In some cases, you could relate the person's experiences to your own to help you understand their point of view. You can use more than just words to learn about your users. You or the users can make drawings, take photos, record quotes, tell stories, draw maps and other images, and visit particular areas in the school community.

Engaging to Build Empathy

Here are some ways to gain empathy and learn about your user:

- **Immerse** **Spend time with your users.**

- **Engage** **Talk to your users and ask questions, such as:**
  - How do you feel about starting in a new school?
  - Why is it difficult for you?
  - What might help make it easier for you to fit in?

  Make notes as you listen to your users.
  - Pay attention to the words they use to describe their experiences.

  Ask follow-up questions to make sure you understand, such as:
  - Tell me more.
  - How do you feel when that happens?

- **Observe** **Watch and listen to your users as they experience their lives.**

Meet some
CHANGE MAKERS

New Students and THINK

Fitting in at a new school can be hard. Fifth- and sixth-graders at Rymfire Elementary School in Palm Coast, Florida, formed a group called THINK, which stands for "To Help Include New Kids." They talked with new students to understand their needs. They learned that new students often feel confused about where to go. They also feel lonely and excluded from the school community. THINK used this information to design a solution.

New students at Rymfire are now given a welcome box of school supplies, a free snack ticket for the cafeteria, and a tour of the school. THINK members schedule times to have lunch or play at recess with new students. They hold "get to know you" events during the year. The THINK team used empathy to design a solution that truly meets the needs of new students.

The THINK team welcomes new students and makes them feel more comfortable in their new surroundings.

Define

Defining the Need

Once you have used empathy to understand your user's point of view, it's time to define their problem, or need. First, review the information you gathered during the empathy stage.

Look for patterns, themes, and big ideas in the information you gathered during the empathy stage. There are many tools you can use to organize your ideas. You could create a timeline of the user's experiences with the problem, or use word pairs such as "important/not important," "often/not often," or "easy/hard" to sort your ideas.

Empathy Map

- Create an empathy map. Start by asking these questions:
  - What words does the user say often when they talk about the problem?
  - How do they act in response to the problem?
  - What do they think about the problem?
  - How do they feel about the problem?
- Draw four quadrants as shown here and fill in what you learned.

Says	Does
Thinks	Feels

To help look for patterns in what they learned, the students in THINK might have asked themselves questions such as, "*What did we learn about new students in our school?*" and "*Did the new students suggest possible solutions that might work?*"

Define a Point of View

A point of view is the way a person in a situation thinks or feels about something. Different people may see the same event differently, depending on their point of view. A **point of view (POV) statement** summarizes who the user is and describes the need from their point of view.

TIPS: Defining POV

To help create a POV statement, the students who formed THINK might have asked themselves:

- Who is the user?
- What needs has the user identified?
- Why does this problem exist?

The THINK group might have written the following POV statement: "New students feel lonely and excluded at our school because they don't know anybody and aren't familiar with the surroundings."

Write a Point of View Question

Writing a **POV question** helps you define a way to solve the problem. The POV question lays out the problem you will try to solve. For example, the THINK group identified new students as the users and the students' need was to feel included in the school community. The group might have created the following POV question to help generate solutions for the problem: "How can we develop a way to help new students feel more included in the school community?"

Good POV statements and questions should accomplish the following:

- Be human centered
- Focus and identify the problem
- Inspire you or your team
- Help you choose which ideas will work and which ones won't
- Encourage you to come up with one solution for one user, rather than multiple solutions for many users
- Capture the heart and minds of others

Getting Started

Use these prompts to help draft a POV question:

- How can we help …?
- How can we create a way to …?
- How can we improve …?
- How can we prevent …?
- How might we …?

Ideate

What Is Ideation?

deation means forming ideas. In this design-thinking step, you will come up with ways to solve the problem. The solution could be a new **product**—a physical or digital creation, or an experience. It could also be a new process, or way of doing things.

Write all your ideas on a whiteboard, chart paper, or on lots of sticky notes.

Some solutions may involve both products and processes. At this stage you will use your imagination and creativity to come up with as many different ideas as you can. Then, you will choose the best ideas to explore further.

For example, the students who started THINK developed both a tool and a process to address how to help new students feel welcomed at school. They created a box of school supplies and other items. They also developed a series of actions to take when new students come to the school, such as taking them on a tour, holding "get to know you" events, and scheduling time to spend with them.

Brainstorm!

Brainstorming is a way of quickly generating lots of ideas. The ideas can be big or small; practical or "out there." At this stage, there are no bad ideas! What might seem silly at first might lead to a very useful solution.

Encourage every member of your team to contribute their ideas. You want to get as wide a range of ideas and suggestions at this stage.

Make sure to record your brainstorming ideas so you can refer back to them later. You could use chart paper or a whiteboard to do this. You can also use words and images such as photos or sketches to record ideas.

TIPS: Brainstorming Tools

- Whiteboards and dry erase markers
- Chalkboard and chalk
- Chart paper and markers
- Sticky notes, scrap paper, or notebooks and pens or pencils

Tip: Set yourself a time limit—perhaps an hour—for deciding on the ideas you will explore more.

Choosing an Idea

Which of your ideas is the strongest? Try these strategies to help you decide:

- Use numbers to rank your ideas by how well you think they will meet the user's need.
- Sort ideas using headings such as "easiest," "cheapest," "most fun," and "long-shots."
- Have team members put stickers beside their 2 or 3 favorite ideas. The idea with the most stickers goes on to the next stage.

Prototype

What Is a Prototype?

To find out if your best idea will work, you need to create a **prototype**. A prototype is a **model** of the idea you chose in the ideate step. You make a prototype to figure out how the users will interact with the idea, what works, and what needs improving.

As you create a prototype, think about its user and his or her problem. Will your prototype meet the user's needs?

If your solution is a product, you might use everyday materials to build a prototype version of it. If your solution is a process, you might create a **storyboard**, video, or use another method to explain how the process works. Keep in mind that your prototype should be simple and easy to create.

You want to be able to easily make changes to your idea for the next version.

Building a Prototype

Prototypes are anything the user can experience or interact with. The following are some different types of prototypes and methods you could use to create them.

- Use paper, craft supplies, or found objects to create a physical object, such as a tool.

If your solution is a website, you can create a storyboard that shows how it might look.

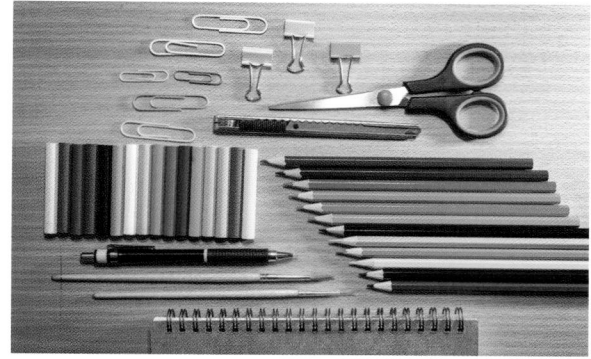

- Use a storyboard, diagram, images, sketches, or flow charts to show a process.
- Create a role-playing scenario or skit by writing or improvising a scene in which you or others step into the user's shoes and try out the solution. You could also act out the scenario using action figures, or watch others act out the scenario and take notes.

- If you want to create a website or other digital solution, use a computer to show others your prototype. Or, draw your website and all of its parts on paper or a large board.

TIPS:
Creating a Prototype
- Prototypes don't have to be pretty and perfect. Revise as you go.
- Set a time limit. Prototypes should be easy to create so you can go back and modify them many times.
- Stay focused on the user and his or her need.

Test

Putting it to the Test

Testing your prototype means letting users try it out. This helps you better understand how well your solution meets your users' needs. It also shows the strengths and weaknesses of your idea.

Testing can include asking users to try out a physical object or watch a video or presentation of an idea or process. You could also ask users to "walk you through" your storyboard. Make sure to use a range of tools, including text and visuals, to make sure the user understands the process.

Testing the prototype gives you valuable information.

Show, don't tell. You want the user to experience the idea. Take notes while you watch, so you will know what you need to change.

Observing the user testing your solution gives you valuable information. You can ask questions about the solutions, and use what you learn to build a better solution, or even change the way you defined the problem. Remember, failing forward is part of the design-thinking process.

The User's Experience

To test your idea, create an experience for the user. Then watch the user try to use or understand your idea. For example:

- Explain your concept and then let the user try the prototype.
- Create an experience for the user that allows them to interact with your object, product, or presentation.
- Although the user should test the prototype, sometimes that is not possible. If the user is not available to try your prototype, have classmates, peers, or others test it. Make sure you tell them what you learned about the user in the empathy stage before you have them step into the user's shoes. Tell them your POV statement and question.

Get Feedback

Getting feedback from the user is crucial. You also need to keep track of the feedback that you receive so you can use it in the next iteration of the process. Some ways of getting feedback are:

- Watch the user interact with your solution. Note or record what you observed.
- Use a survey to collect as much feedback as possible from groups of users.
- Ask follow-up questions:
  - What do you like about it?
  - What questions do you have?
  - What changes would you make?
  - How can we improve the experience?

If your prototype doesn't work as you expected, use what you learned to build a better solution. Remember, it is okay to fail forward.

Reflect

Reflecting on Results

Reflection is part of the each step in the design-thinking process. At every stage, you gather information, think about it, and make improvements. However, the final step in design thinking is focused entirely on reflection. It is time to think about what you have learned so far and decide what comes next.

Start by going back to the empathy and define steps in the process. How well does your idea solve the problem you defined? How well does it meet the needs of the user? Do any needs still need to be met? How well did testing your prototype help you answer these questions?

Discuss with a group what you learned during the reflection stage. You can learn a lot by listening to others' ideas and reflections.

TIPS:
Reflection Strategies

- List the strengths and weaknesses of your prototype. What still needs work?
- Jot down any new ideas that came to you during testing. Could they help you improve your solution?
- Talk to peers about what you learned and discovered during the design-thinking process.
- Record your reflections in a journal entry, drawings, or a video or slide show.

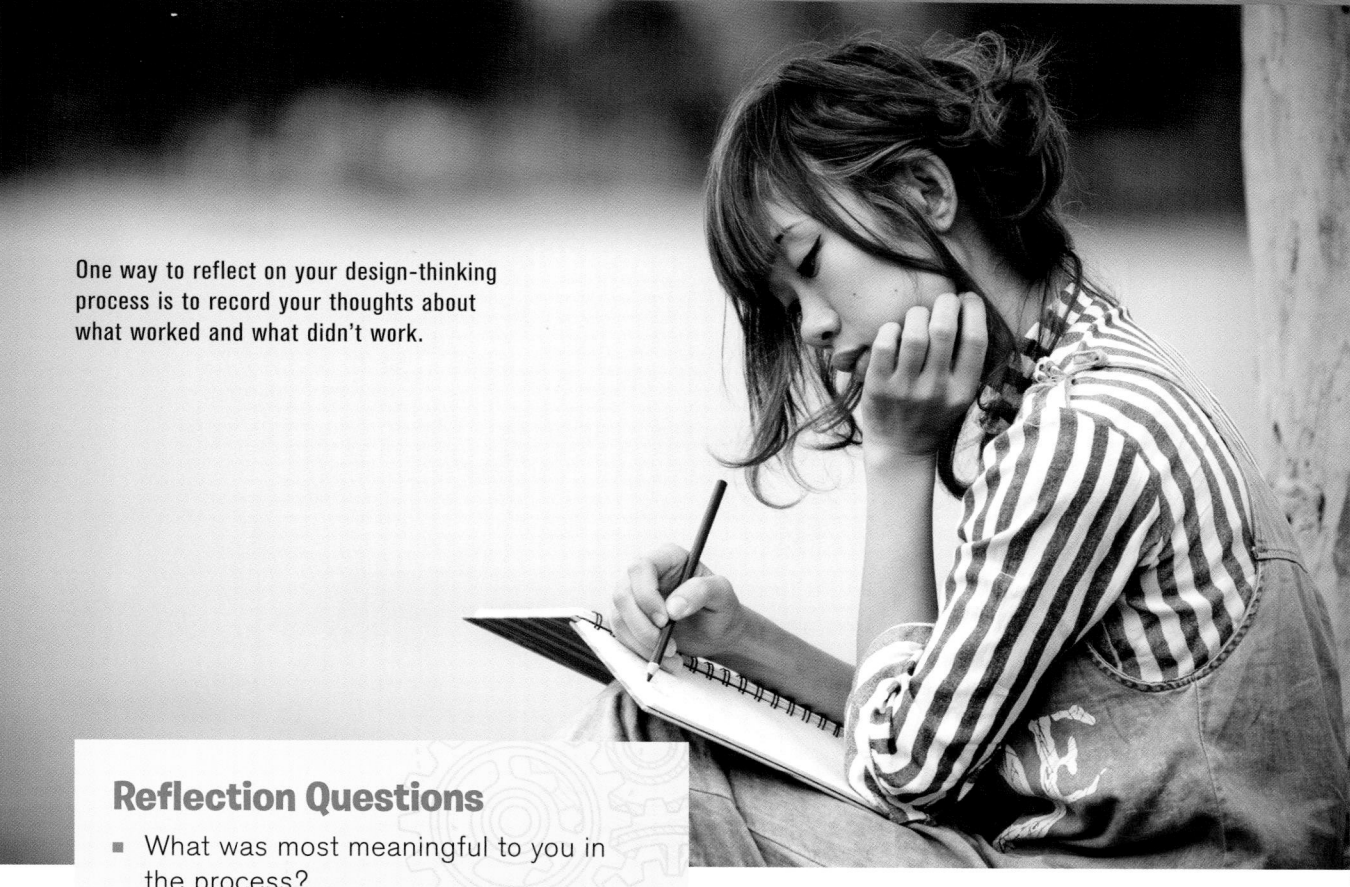

One way to reflect on your design-thinking process is to record your thoughts about what worked and what didn't work.

Reflection Questions

- What was most meaningful to you in the process?
- What personal strengths or areas for improvement did you discover?
- What changed what you thought? Did anything confirm your original ideas?
- What worked well? What will you do differently next time?
- What did others think of your solution?

Your answers to the reflection questions will help you plan your next steps.

Document and Present Your Results

Provide a short summary of the experience that describes each step and the tools you used. You could write a journal entry or create a slide show, web page, or video. You could also create a drawing, illustrate a story, or write and perform a poem or song.

Include your own observations and your users' feedback. State your conclusions and highlight how the information you gathered illustrates these conclusions. Then, make recommendations for what you will do next.

What Comes Next?

Use what you learned from the reflection step and make plans for the next step. Are you ready to put the solution into action? Or does it need improvement? Remember that the design-thinking process is iterative. Repeat the steps in the design-thinking process if you need to create a better solution.

PROJECT:

Challenges for New Students

Have you ever changed schools? Maybe you came to your current school from another one in your neighborhood. Or perhaps your family moved to your community from another town, city, or country.

If you were lucky, other students welcomed and helped you, and you soon had new friends. Before long you felt at home and a part of your new school community. But too often, new students face a number of challenges—from being uncomfortable in a new and unfamiliar setting, to feeling lonely and disconnected from peers. Some new students experience **prejudice** and **discrimination**, often when their culture or beliefs differ from the common ones at their new school.

Where Does Prejudice Come From?

Ignorance → Fear → Prejudice

Many people are scared of new things or of things they don't understand or are ignorant about. This fear can lead to prejudice. To be prejudiced is to have unfriendly feelings directed against a person or a group of people without good reason.

For new students, schools can be unfamiliar and overwhelming. A friendly peer can help new students navigate such things as crowded hallways.

Everyone needs a safe, stress-free environment for learning. When new students feel uncomfortable with their new environment, their health, academic performance, and social life are negatively affected. A positive school community is one in which all students—including newcomers—feel safe and are included.

- Students may not know where to go or what to do on their first day at a new school. They may feel lonely because they don't know anyone. They don't know the school's routines or schedules and may get lost.

- Students may face challenges when they start at a new school because people at the school are unfamiliar with their language, culture, or religion. Sometimes, unfamiliarity or ignorance can lead to prejudice and discrimination.

- Students who speak a different language, or who are not yet comfortable speaking the language spoken at school, may have difficulty communicating with teachers and other students at a new school. This can harm their social life and ability to learn.

Payton Klein and The Global Minds Initiative

Meet a
CHANGE
MAKER

Students in Payton Klein's high school speak 16 different languages. Payton believed this amazing diversity should be celebrated, but instead she saw that students new to the school were being excluded from school experiences because they didn't yet speak English. She also observed how new classmates who were still learning English often struggled to communicate with teachers and other students.

Payton spoke to new students in her school to learn about their needs. She learned that new students wanted to improve their English skills, but needed help from others to learn. She designed a weekly after-school program called Global Minds. The program pairs new students with peers for tutoring sessions. Pairs also participate together in community service activities centered around human rights, diversity, and ways to encourage people from different backgrounds to work together and understand each other. Global Minds helps new students succeed in learning English and feel included, and encourages all students to build global leadership skills and celebrate diversity.

The Global Minds Initiative helps new students feel welcome in their new school.

Navigating a New School

Gillian is a new student in ninth grade at a large city school. She moved to the area with her family during the summer because of her mother's job. Her new school is much bigger than the one she attended in her small hometown. She feels nervous and alone at her new school as she tries to figure out the new routines and find her way around. She is worried that the schoolwork will be harder at her new school, and that she will have trouble keeping up. Finding her way around the school, trying to fit in, and making friends are other stressful and challenging tasks for Gillian. She used to really enjoy school at her old home. But now Gillian feels overwhelmed and dreads going to school.

Gillian's experience is not unique.
Moving to a new school can be overwhelming.

- More than 6.5 million students in the United States change schools every year.

- According to a recent survey of 600 students, students starting at a new school are most worried about schoolwork, fitting in, having friends, being judged or teased, and appearance.

- A 2015 study found that the number of times students move to a new school is related to their achievement. The more often students move, the lower their scores on standardized tests.

The Design-thinking Process

Empathy What challenges does Gillian face as a new student? How does it make her feel?

Define POV After you have used empathy to understand Gillian's point of view, define her needs. Create a POV question that helps you begin to solve her problem.

POV QUESTION PROMPT: **How can we help... ?**

CASE

Connecting with New Peers

Juan Pablo is a Colombian **refugee** who moved to Canada with his family during the summer. Juan Pablo's family fled from Colombia to escape the violence of civil war and lived in a refugee camp for many years before being granted a permanent home in Canada. Juan Pablo was nervous to start the school year because Canada is so different from what he is used to. He wants to feel part of his new school community, but it is difficult because he speaks very little English. His new school is much bigger than what he is used to. Because he is still learning English, he finds the rules very confusing and sometimes breaks them accidentally. He has no friends yet and feels bored and lonely. He wishes he had someone to talk to about his life back home and his scary experience of escaping war.

Although many students welcome refugees, it can still be difficult for them to fit in at their new schools.

Most refugees had to flee their home country because of a war. They often live in refugee camps, such as the one to the right, in neighboring countries for many years while they wait to be accepted into another country. Many refugee parents hope to move with their families to Europe or North America so their children can get a good education.

Around the world, refugees like Juan Pablo face challenges when starting at a new school.

- In 2016, 300,000 immigrants and 47,000 refugees came to Canada. Between 2000 and 2014, 18.7 million new immigrants and 800,000 refugees settled in the United States.

- Many schools have English as a Second Language programs to help students like Juan Pablo learn English. These programs usually have special teachers who spend extra time with students to develop their speaking, writing, and reading skills.

- Research shows that making friends helps new students adjust to school and learn the language.

The Design-thinking Process

Empathy What is making it difficult for Juan Pablo to feel like he is part of his school community? How does this make Juan Pablo feel?

Define POV After you have used empathy to understand Juan Pablo's point of view, define his needs. Create a POV question that helps you begin to solve his problem.

POV QUESTION PROMPT: **How can we improve ... ?**

CASE

Cultural Challenges

Mustafa is a **Muslim** student in eighth grade, who has just moved to a new school with very few other Muslim students. Muslims like Mustafa **observe** **Ramadan** for one month every year, which includes fasting, or not eating, from sunrise to sunset. Mustafa also must pray at times throughout the school day.

But it is challenging for him to follow his religious practices at school. Mustafa finds it difficult to spend lunch hour with other students who are all eating. He feels frustrated that there are no quiet places available for him to pray. Sometimes, Mustafa ends up staying home because there isn't a safe place in the school to pray or spend the lunch hour.

But he doesn't want to be away from his learning and his new friends. The school does not have any plans in place to help him observe Ramadan and attend class as usual.

Schools can support Muslim students by providing a quiet space for them to pray during the day.

There are many students like Mustafa across North America.

- In 2015, about 3.3 million Muslims of all ages were living in the United States. Most people start fasting for Ramadan at age 12. This means many school-aged children are fasting during their school day.

- Many schools are putting plans in place to support students who fast for Ramadan. For example, schools may provide space for Muslim students to spend lunch and break time away from students who are eating. Schools can also plan special events around Ramadan, such as sports days or rewards lunches.

- Young people often fast as a way of empathizing with the disadvantaged. When asked why she fasts, one young girl said, "We're trying to feel what they're feeling. They don't have food, don't have a house…"

 ## The Design-thinking Process

Empathy What barriers stop Mustafa from comfortably practicing his religion at his new school? How does this affect him? How does this make him feel?

Define POV After you have used empathy to understand Mustafa's point of view,, define his needs. Create a POV question that helps you begin to solve his problem.

POV QUESTION PROMPT: **How can we make it possible for … ?**

Welcoming New Students

How might we make sure all students feel welcome and valued in the school community?

Now it's your turn to make a difference! Use the design-thinking process to create a solution to a problem that new students experience in your school community.

Start by thinking about the three users who are facing challenges at their new school:

1. Gillian is attending a new school that is much bigger than her old one. She feels unsure in her new surroundings and does not know how to make new friends.

2. Juan Pablo is new to a school and is having difficulty connecting with peers and understanding new school rules and practices, because he does not speak English.

3. Mustafa is facing challenges observing Ramadan at his new school, where there are very few Muslim students.

Which student would you like to help? Choose either Gillian, Juan Pablo, or Mustafa's case and use the design-thinking steps to create a solution to their problem.

Empathize

Empathize to learn more about the user's point of view:
- Ask questions about their needs.
- Learn more by watching videos and reading articles.

Define

Use the POV prompt from the case study to define the user's need.

Ideate

It's time to brainstorm! Draw, sketch, or write down as many ideas as possible. Organize your ideas and select one for the next stage.

Prototype

Create a prototype of your idea—keep it simple and inexpensive. Remember that your prototype should be something the user can experience.

Test

Show, don't tell—have someone experience your prototype. Observe your user's experience with the prototype and take notes on what works and what doesn't work.

Reflect

Reflect on the results of your test
- Has your prototype met the needs of the user?
- What can you change?

Reflect on the design-thinking process.
- What did you learn?
- What could you do differently?

Now, improve your prototype through another iteration of the process. When you are happy with your solution, share it with your peers.

PROJECT:

Accessibility in School Communities

In the United States and Canada, elementary and secondary schools are required by law to accommodate students of all abilities. This may include having accessible buildings for students who have physical disabilities or creating individual learning plans for students who have learning disabilities.

But even with the accommodations schools make, students with different abilities often feel that their schools are not fully **inclusive**.

Schools often don't have access to extra equipment and supplies to meet the social, emotional, and sometimes physical needs of students with different abilities. Students with physical disabilities may need special sports equipment so they can participate fully in school activities. This equipment is often expensive. Other students may need a quiet place in the school where they can go when they are feeling overwhelmed by their surroundings. Many schools don't have extra space to set up this type of safe place for students. And some students with different abilities may face prejudice and discrimination from others because they are different. They need students and teachers to understand them and their needs.

With special equipment and other accommodations, students with physical disabilities can play soccer and participate in other sports.

It is important to address the challenges faced by students with different abilities to ensure they succeed and are not left behind. Some of these challenges include:

- Students with physical disabilities may want to participate in a variety of activities but can't because the school does not have the equipment or spaces that make those activities accessible.
- Students with different **cognitive** abilities, such as those on the **autism spectrum**, may not feel connected to others at school because teachers and students don't understand how to help and interact with them. As they sometimes communicate differently, social connections at school can be a challenge.
- Students with different abilities may face prejudice and discrimination from students and teachers who may misunderstand or misrepresent their abilities.

Creating Accessible Playgrounds

Meet some CHANGE MAKERS

Owen Chaidez from Chicago uses a wheelchair to get around. When he tried to use the playground at his school, the wheels of his wheelchair became stuck in the wood chips on the surface of the play area. He felt like he was being left on the sidelines at recess. Owen's mother saw how upset he was at not being able to use the playground and vowed to make a difference. She worked with other parents and nonprofit organizations to solve the problem.

Together, they designed and built "Owen's Playground." This fully accessible playground is designed to be used by all students, including those with disabilities. The playground has extra-wide ramps that fit wheelchairs, swings with bucket seats, which hold students with all physical abilities on the swing, and sensory stations, which help students explore their senses and keep calm. It also has a rubberized surface instead of wood chips so wheelchairs don't get stuck. All students at the school use the playground every day, and visitors from the area use the playground after school hours. Now, Owen and every student can participate on the playground at recess.

Accessible playgrounds allow all children to participate.

CASE

Different Abilities and Sports

Anna is a student in sixth grade who has a **visual impairment**. She is functionally blind, which means she has limited vision and needs to use her hearing and sense of touch for learning. Baseball is a popular sport at Anna's school, and she really wants to play. However, her teachers say she can't because of her visual impairment. They explain that baseball is not safe for her. Anna is frustrated.

She knows some other schools have figured out ways for students with visual impairments to participate in different sports and wonders why her school won't help her participate too. She feels left out and sad that she can't play baseball with her classmates.

Beepball is a form of baseball where players wear blindfolds. The batter tries to hit a beeping ball off a tee, then runs to a beeping base, which is about the size of a football tackling dummy. They try to make it to the base before fielders track down the ball. The beeping noise helps people who cannot see figure out where to go.

Students with visual impairments like Anna face a variety of challenges in school.

- Experts estimate that about 100,000 students in the United States have a visual impairment.

- A 2000 survey of young people with disabilities indicated that over 25% had not participated in any sports in the last year, compared to 6% of young people without disabilities.

- The survey identified the following barriers to participation in sports for young people with disabilities: lack of money, unsuitable sports facilities, unwelcoming staff at facilities, and lack of accommodation for their needs.

The Design-thinking Process

Empathy How is Anna affected by not being able to participate in baseball at her school? How does it make her feel?

Define POV After you have used empathy to understand Anna's point of view, define her needs. Create a POV question that helps you begin to solve her problem.

POV QUESTION PROMPT: **How can we help… ?**

CASE

Autism and Communication

Nathan is a ninth-grader who has autism spectrum disorder. He has difficulty communicating with others in a social environment and doesn't feel connected to the other students at school. He also displays repetitive behaviors and struggles with loud noises and changes in routine. As a result, Nathan has few friends and has been bullied because he is different. There are no safe and quiet places in his school where he can go when he is feeling overwhelmed. The classroom is often too chaotic for him to focus. Teachers and other students aren't sure how to accommodate or help him in the classroom. Nathan isn't doing well in his classes, and he feels frustrated that nobody at school understands what he needs.

No two people who have autism are alike. Autism looks different in different people, so solutions that help people with autism need to be unique to them.

Nathan is not alone. Many students with autism face challenges at school.

- Autism affects 1 in 68 children in the United States.
- Students with autism experience a number of challenges when communicating with others. They often have difficulty understanding what others are saying, and they may have difficulty developing language skills. They also often have trouble with nonverbal communication, such as hand gestures, eye contact, and facial expressions.
- People with autism have difficulty understanding the feelings of others. As one person describes, "I have so much trouble seeing the world the way you do."

The Design-thinking Process

Empathy How does Nathan feel in his school community? What barriers stop him from functioning and doing well at school?

Define POV After you have used empathy to understand Nathan's point of view, define his needs. Create a POV question that helps you begin to solve his problem.

POV QUESTION PROMPT: **How can we make it easier for … ?**

CASE

Cerebral Palsy and Participation

Megan is a student in seventh grade who has **cerebral palsy**. She sometimes has trouble getting around the school because she uses a wheelchair and not all of her school is accessible. As a result, she can't participate in all the activities that she wants to. Some teachers have low expectations of what she can do and don't include her in the regular classroom activities. Megan feels that people forget that she has the same learning abilities and social interests as other students. Classmates rarely ask Megan to be their partner in group work. She feels left out from the school community. Megan has also been bullied because she is different. Some students have made fun of her wheelchair or posted mean jokes about her online.

Schools are not always accessible for students who need to use a wheelchair. Items that are left on the ground, such as the skipping rope shown here, can prevent wheelchair users from getting around safely and easily.

Students like Megan who have a physical disability often face challenges in school.

- About 500,000 children and adults in the United States have cerebral palsy.
- People with cerebral palsy have difficulty controlling their muscles. Many need a wheelchair to get around. Cerebral palsy can also affect hearing, seeing, and thinking. CP looks different in different people. No two people with cerebral palsy are exactly alike.
- People with cerebral palsy often use special equipment to help them perform everyday tasks.

 **The Design-thinking Process**

Empathy How is Megan affected by the way students and teachers treat her? How do these challenges make her feel?

Define POV After you have used empathy to understand Megan's point of view, define her needs. Create a POV question that helps you begin to solve her problem.

POV QUESTION PROMPT: **How can we create a way to... ?**

Design Thinking in Practice

Different Abilities

How might we make sure all school communities are accessible for every student?

Now it's your turn to make a difference! Use the design-thinking process to ensure your school is accessible for a person, a group, or a community.

Think about the three users with different abilities who are facing challenges in their school community:

1. Anna, a student with a visual impairment, wants to be able to participate in baseball like the other students. She feels frustrated that her school has not worked to help her participate.

2. Nathan, a student with autism spectrum disorder, faces barriers to communicating with others at school. His learning is also impacted because he finds his classroom very chaotic.

3. Megan, a student with cerebral palsy, feels left out from the school community. She feels that her classmates misunderstand her disability.

Most students with different physical and mental abilities are just like other students. They enjoy the same things, and want to participate in the same activities.

34

Choose either Anna, Nathan, or Megan's case and use the design-thinking steps to create a solution to their problem.

Empathize

Empathize to learn more about the user's point of view:
- Examine their stories, challenges, and frustrations.
- Learn more by watching videos and reading articles.

Define

Use the POV prompt from the case study to define the user's need.

Ideate

It's time to brainstorm! Draw, sketch, or write down as many ideas as possible. Organize your ideas and select one for the next stage.

Prototype

Create a prototype of your idea—keep it simple and inexpensive. Remember that your prototype should be an experience.

Test

Show, don't tell—have your peers test your prototype and give you feedback.

Reflect

Reflect on the results of your test
- Has your prototype met the needs of the user?
- What can you change?

Reflect on the design-thinking process.
- What did you learn?
- What could you do differently?

Now, improve your prototype through another iteration of the process. When you are happy with your solution, share it with your peers.

PROJECT:

Bullying at School

Have you ever encountered a bully? You're not alone. Experts report that more than half of all students experience some form of bullying. Bullying in schools can happen in the hallway, cafeteria, classroom, or schoolyard, on the school bus, or on computers or smartphones.

No matter where it happens, bullying affects the entire school community by making it a negative place to be. Positive school communities are bully-free. Teachers, supervisors, and students all play a role in getting involved and intervening to reduce bullying in schools.

All students should feel safe in school. Being bullied is one big way that students feel unsafe and isolated in their school community.

Bullying takes many forms:
- Verbal bullying involves name-calling, insults, threats, or inappropriate comments.
- Social bullying refers to spreading rumors about someone, with the goal of excluding them or embarrassing them in front of others.

- Physical bullying involves pushing, tripping, pinching, or hitting someone, or damaging their property.
- Cyberbullying includes abusive or hurtful emails, texts, posts, or online videos.

Students are bullied for many different reasons. These can include the way that they look and their **race** or **ethnicity**—especially if it is different from the majority of others at the school. Other students could experience bullying because of their religion or culture. For immigrant and refugee students, this can make them feel isolated from peers at a new school. Other reasons for bullying might include someone's **gender** or **sexuality**, or their parents' income. The peak years for bullying are in grades 7, 8, and 9.

How Bullying Affects People

Bullying creates a negative and unsafe environment. Students who are bullied are likely to experience negative effects in other parts of their lives, such as their learning at school or how healthy they feel. Bullied students might:

- Do poorly in school
- Feel disconnected from or dislike their school
- Suffer from a **mental illness** such as **depression** or **anxiety**
- Feel lonely
- Lack friendships
- Have low self-esteem
- Experience nightmares
- Have stomachaches and headaches

Jaylens Challenge

When Jaylen Arnold was 8 years old, he decided he wanted to make a difference. Jaylen has Tourette Syndrome, which means that he makes uncontrollable sounds and movements. Jaylen was bullied for months at school because he was different. From personal experience, he knew the effects of bullying. He also learned that other bullied children, like him, did not know how to help stop the problem. Jaylen decided that he needed to find a solution for bullied children who didn't have anyone to help them or who didn't know how to help themselves.

Jaylen discussed the problem with his parents. He decided that he would try to educate others on the effects of bullying and how to stop it, so that children everywhere would know how to get help and also how to help others. He started by creating a simple website that educated his classmates on the effects of bullying. He wanted to teach the bullies the effects they were having on others. Then, he started spreading his anti-bullying message to a wider audience. Jaylen has been featured on newscasts and TV shows and in magazines. His foundation, Jaylens Challenge, provides videos, printed materials, and lesson plans to schools to educate teachers and students about bullying.

Meet a CHANGE MAKER

37

Verbal Bullying

Marisela is a student in sixth grade. She is bullied on the playground and in other areas outside of the classroom because she is quiet and shy. She finds it hard to stand up for herself. The bullies call her names and make fun of her. She cries every day when she gets home, and her stomach hurts every morning when she thinks about going back to school. Marisela feels like she can't tell her parents about what is happening because they have too many other things to worry about. She wants to talk to someone, but doesn't know who. She worries that telling someone at school will make things worse. She knows she needs some strategies and tools to help her deal with bullying, but doesn't know how to learn them.

The awareness of the effects of bullying is growing around the world. Students, parents, and school staff are working to make schools a safe place that is free of bullying.

Marisela is not alone. Children all around the world are the victims of bullying.

- In a study of 80,000 students across the United States, 25% said they had been bullied. Other studies report that more than half of all students have been bullied.

- A 2013 Canadian study reported that name-calling and insults are the most common form of bullying.

- Interviews with students show that students don't report bullying because they don't want their parents to overreact or worry, they feel ashamed, or they don't think that anyone will listen.

The Design-thinking Process

Empathy How is Marisela affected by being bullied in school? How does being bullied make her feel?

Define POV After you have used empathy to understand Marisela's point of view, define her needs. Create a POV question that helps you begin to solve her problem.

POV QUESTION PROMPT: **How can we prevent … ?**

CASE

Cyberbullying

Ahmed is a ninth grader who loves math. His teacher knows he will always have the correct answer to math questions and often calls on him in class. But Ahmed is being cyberbullied by some of his classmates. They text him at all hours of the day and night, threatening to beat him up for being the teacher's pet. They accuse him of getting special treatment from the teacher and say he doesn't deserve his good grades. Because cyberbullies have access to their smartphones 24/7, Ahmed has no way to escape from their bullying. He is starting to think that doing well at math isn't such a good thing. He feels anxious all the time, and doesn't know how to make the bullying stop. He knows he should talk to somebody, but he's scared of what may happen. The cyberbullies threatened to beat up his younger brother too if he tells anyone.

Research shows that people who are cyberbullied are more likely to experience depression. Boys are more likely than girls to be cyberbullies.

Ahmed's experience is not unique. Cyberbullying is becoming more common in North America.

- More than 1 in 4 students have been bullied online.
- 70% of students in the United States say they often see cases of online bullying.
- Like Ahmed, people who are cyberbullied feel discouraged and scared. As one victim said, "I cried multiple times. I could't let it go. I questioned my value as a person. I was angry."

The Design-thinking Process

Empathy How is Ahmed affected by cyberbullying? How does being cyberbullied make him feel?

Define POV After you have used empathy to understand Ahmed's point of view, define his needs. Create a POV question that helps you begin to solve his problem.

POV QUESTION PROMPT: **How can we help ... ?**

CASE

Socal Bullying

Farah is an immigrant from Haiti who is in ninth grade. She has been bullied since she moved to the United States two years ago. She is shy, which makes it hard for her to make new friends. The other students leave her out of activities. She has never been invited to spend time with her peers outside of school. They sometimes make fun of her because she is from another country, looks and dresses differently from them, and has an accent when she speaks English. She tried to talk to her teachers about the problem, but nothing changed.

Victims of social bullying often feel rejected, unwanted, or isolated.

The bullies now hide their behavior from the teachers. With no one to stand up for her and no friends to talk to, Farah feels isolated and alone. She does not trust her peers. She doesn't know who to talk to at the school to get help. She feels stressed and anxious most of the time.

Bullying can make newcomers feel frightened and insecure. Schools can help by educating students, staff, and parents about how to prevent bullying.

Many immigrants like Farah are the victims of bullying.

- In 2017, 23% of public school students in the United States were from immigrant families. In 1990, only 11% of students were immigrants.
- According to a 2017 study, immigrant and refugee children are more likely to be bullied than those born in the United States.
- The same study indicated that male immigrant and refugee children are more likely than female children to experience bullying related to their religion or race and cyberbullying.

 ## The Design-thinking Process

Empathy How does bullying make Farah feel? How does being bullied affect her experience in her new country?

Define POV After you have used empathy to understand Farah's point of view, define her needs. Create a POV question that helps you begin to solve her problem.

POV QUESTION PROMPT: **How can we prevent … ?**

Preventing and Stopping Bullying

How can we stop bullying at school?

Now it's your turn to make a difference! You will work through the design-thinking process to come up with a solution to stop a person or group from being bullied in your school community.

Start by thinking about the three users facing problems in this section:

1. Marisela is experiencing verbal bullying outside of the classroom. She is too shy and afraid to stand up for herself, which only makes the bullying worse.

2. Ahmed is being cyberbullied because his classmates think he is the "teacher's pet" and is getting special treatment.

3. Farah, an immigrant student, is being left out of social activities because she is different from the rest of the students at her school.

Students can help prevent and stop bullying by standing up for others and getting involved in their community.

Which student would you like to help? Choose either Marisela, Ahmed, or Farah's case and use the design-thinking steps to create a solution to their problem.

Empathize

Empathize to learn more about the user's point of view:
- Ask questions about their needs.
- Examine their stories, challenges, and frustrations.

Define

Use the POV prompt from the case study to define the user's need.

Ideate

It's time to brainstorm! Draw, sketch, or write down as many ideas as possible. Organize your ideas and select one for the next stage.

Prototype

Create a prototype of your idea—keep it simple and inexpensive. Remember that your prototype should be an experience.

Test

Show, don't tell—have your peers test your prototype and give you feedback.

Reflect

Reflect on the results of your test
- Has your prototype met the needs of the user?
- What can you change?

Reflect on the design-thinking process.
- What did you learn?
- What could you do differently?

Now, improve your prototype through another iteration of the process. When you are happy with your solution, share it with your peers.

What's Next for Design Thinking?

Today's design thinkers find inspiration everywhere. Look around your school to find ideas on how to make it a more positive community. Remember, small actions can have big consequences!

Get Involved in Design Thinking

Students throughout the United States and Canada are using design thinking to create more positive school communities. The BULLY Project provides resources and ideas to help you start an anti-bullying campaign at school. Trisha Prabhu stepped into the point of view of cyberbullies to create ReThink™, a technology that detects and stops cyberbullying before it starts. A group of 65 students in Winnipeg, Manitoba, raised $300 to replace the lost headphones of a classmate, Gavin Ramsay, who has autism and who relies on music to help manage everyday stresses. Opportunities to apply design thinking don't have to change the entire world—just your corner of it!

Next Steps: Designing for Accessibility

Think about something that interests you about making your school community more positive. What are you passionate about? What problem would you like to solve? Who could you work with to help you solve the problem? Join a group that is interested in promoting a positive school community. You can also read books and do online research about how to stop bullying, how to make schools more accessible to students with different abilities, and how to welcome new students to the school. Learn what others have done and what they are doing today. Think about how you could modify these ideas in your own school community.

By finding ways to meet the needs of the students in your school, you can help create a more positive school community.

Learning More

Design-thinking Guide
A guide for schools developed by Design for Change, an organization that believes children can drive change in their community.
designthinkingguide.weebly.com

Global Minds Initiative
Strategies and resources for creating change in the world.
http://globalminds.world/

IDEAco
A nonprofit organization that helps people become change makers.
www.ideaco.org

PREVNet
A nonprofit organization that provides research and resources for bullying prevention.
www.prevnet.ca

PsychCentral
Strategies to help students adjust to a new school.
https://psychcentral.com/lib/when-you're-the-new-kid-in-school/

Rick Hansen Foundation
A nonprofit organization that provides resources about accessibility issues, information on spinal cord injury. research, and tools for building inclusive playgrounds
https://www.rickhansen.com/Our-Work

Synapse
A resource that provides information about autism, Asperger's syndrome, and related disorders.
https://autism-help.org/index.htm

United Cerebral Palsy
An organization that educates, advocates, and provides resources for people with disabilities.
http://ucp.org/

Bibliography

Introductory Material

"Design Thinking Guide." Design For Change. http://design-thinkingguide.weebly.com/

Follett, Jonathan. "What Is Design Thinking?" December 20, 2016. O'Reilly Media. https://www.oreilly.com/ideas/what-is-design-thinking

Global Minds Initiative. 2017. "About Global Minds." http://globalminds.world/about-global-minds/

Kreinbring, Lisa. "What Is Design Thinking?" June 19, 2015. Henry Ford Learning Institute. https://hfli.org/what-is-design-thinking/

ReThink. http://www.rethinkwords.org/

Project 1: Challenges for New Students

Boorstein, Michelle. "Muslim Children Join Their Parents in Fasting for Ramadan." The Washington Post. July 6, 2014. https://www.washingtonpost.com/local/muslim-children-join-their-parents-in-fasting-for-ramadan/2014/07/06/275ed64e-02ea-11e4-8fd0-3a663dfa68ac_story.html?utm_term=.04ca9f6188a4

Estes, Jacque. "Rymfire Roadrunner THINK Team Takes New Students Under Its Wings." PalmCoastObserver.com. February 3, 2017. https://www.palmcoastobserver.com/photo-gallery/rymfire-roadrunner-t-h-i-n-k-team-takes-new-students-under-their-wings

Griffith, Glenn. "Shen High School Providing Space for Ramadan Observance." Saratogian News. May 26, 2017. http://www.saratogian.com/general-news/20170526/shen-high-school-providing-space-for-ramadan-observance

Kilman, Carrie. "Lonely Language Learners?" Teaching Tolerance. 2009. https://www.tolerance.org/magazine/spring-2009/lonely-language-learners

Leutert, Stephanie. "Dispatches: Ecuador's Invisible Refugee Population." Americas Quarterly. Winter 2012. http://www.americasquarterly.org/node/3281

Puzic, Sonja. "Record Number of Refugees Admitted to Canada in 2016." CTVNews.ca. April 24, 2017. https://www.ctvnews.ca/canada/record-number-of-refugees-admitted-to-canada-in-2016-highest-since-1980-1.3382444

Rappaport, Julia. "What's Your Story?" Facing History and Ourselves. 2017. https://www.facinghistory.org/get-to-know-us/stories/whats-your-story-facing-history-students-give-voice-immigration-experience-documentary-films

"Refugees Arriving in the U.S. from 1990 to 2016." Statista. 2018. https://www.statista.com/statistics/200061/number-of-refugees-arriving-in-the-us/

Sparks, Sarah D. "Student Mobility: How it Affects Learning." Education Week. August 11, 2016. https://www.edweek.org/ew/issues/student-mobility/index.html#affect

Project 2: Accessibility in School Communities

"All about Autism: Autism Quick Facts." American Autism Association. https://www.myautism.org/all-about-autism/autism-quick-facts/

"Autism Prevalence." Autism Speaks. https://www.autismspeaks.org/what-autism/prevalence

Dow, Katherine. "Winnipeg Teens Raise Funds to Replace Headphones for Classmate Living with Autism." CTV News Winnipeg. May 2, 2017. https://winnipeg.ctvnews.ca/winnipeg-teens-raise-funds-to-replace-headphones-for-classmate-living-with-autism-1.3395306

Fernandez, Clarizza. "How to Create an Accessible Infographic." Access IQ. September 27, 2012. http://www.accessiq.org/create/content/how-to-create-an-accessible-infographic

"Let Me Tell You about My Autism." Synapse. Autistic Spectrum Disorders Fact Sheets. https://autism-help.org/tell-you-autism-asperger%27s.htm

Ortiz Healy, Vikki. "Parents, Nonprofits Unite to Create More Inclusive Playgrounds for Disabled." Chicago Tribune. September 11, 2016. http://www.chicagotribune.com/news/ct-playgrounds-for-everyone-met-20160911-story.html

"Report Reveals that Disabled Children Take Part in Less Sport than Their Able-Bodied Counterparts." College Sports Scholarships. 2018. https://www.collegesportsscholarships.com/disabled-children-sports.htm

"Take Me Out to the Beep Baseball Game." Braille-Works. April 9, 2013. https://brailleworks.com/beep-baseball/

"Visual Impairments." Project Ideal. http://www.projectidealonline.org/v/visual-impairments/

"What Is Cerebral Palsy?" United Cerebral Palsy. http://ucp.org/wp-content/uploads/2013/01/What-is-CP-Brochure-01_09_14.pdf

Project 3: Bullying at School

"11 Facts About Cyber Bullying." DoSomething.org. https://www.dosomething.org/us/facts/11-facts-about-cyber-bullying

"Bullying No Way!" Jaylens Challenge. http://www.jaylenschallenge.org/

"Canada Bullying Statistics." Stop a Bully. http://www.stopabully.ca/bullying-statistics.html

Caravita, Simona C. "Migrant and Refugee Children Face Higher Rates of Bullying." Unicef. October 12, 2016. https://blogs.unicef.org/evidence-for-action/migrant-children-face-higher-rates-of-bullying/

Foster, Melody Harstine. "High School Students Putting an End to Bullying in Their School via @WestHighBros." Twitchange. March 5, 2013. http://twitchange.com/high-school-students-putting-an-end-to-bullying-in-their-school-via-westhighbros/

Hirschstein, Miriam. "Why Don't Kids Report Bullying?" education.com. May 20, 2009. https://www.education/reference/article/why-kids-do-not-report-bullying/

Kekarpman. "Bullying Based on Assumptions: Immigrant Student Interactions in American Schools." Children of Immigration. December 15, 2014. http://pages.vassar.edu/children-of-immigration/2014/12/15/bullying-based-on-assumptions-immigrant-student-interactions-in-american-schools/

Maynard, Brandy R., Michael G. Vaughn, Christopher P. Salas-Wright, and Sharon R. Vaughn. "Bullying Victimization among School-Aged Immigrant Youth in the United States." Journal of Adolescent Health. March 2016. https://www.ncbi.nlm.nih.gov/pmc/articles/PMC4764796/

"Promoting Relationships and Eliminating Violence Network." PREVNet. http://www.prevnet.ca/about

"Reasons Teens Don't Tell." Teens Against Bullying. https://pacerteensagainstbullying.org/experiencing-bullying/reasons-teens-dont-tell/

Riggio, Ronald E. "Are You an Easy Target for Bullies?" Psychology Today. January 3, 2013. https://www.psychologytoday.com/blog/cutting-edge-leadership/201301/are-you-easy-target-bullies

"Self-Esteem and Cyberbullying." Cyberbullying Research Center. September 24, 2010. https://cyberbullying.org/self-esteem-and-cyberbullying

"Stop a Bully Statistics since 2009." Stop a Bully. http://www.stopabully.ca/program-statistics.html

The Bully Project. http://www.thebullyproject.com/

Vitoroulis, Irene, Heather Brittain, and Tracy Vaillancourt. "School Ethnic Composition and Bullying in Canadian Schools." International Journal of Behavioral Development. September 30, 2015. http://citeseerx.ist.psu.edu/viewdoc/download?doi=10.1.1.858.2022&rep=rep1&type=pdf

"What is the Relationship Between Shyness and Bullying?" NOBullying.com. December 22, 2015. https://nobullying.com/shyness/

"What Stresses You Out About School?" TeensHealth. http://kidshealth.org/en/teens/school-stress.html?WT.ac=t-ra

Glossary

anxiety Feeling scared or nervous, or a condition in which a person feels scared or nervous all the time

autism spectrum A condition in which people have difficulty forming relationships and communicating with others

brainstorming A group discussion that generates ideas

cerebral palsy A disease where a person has difficulty moving and speaking

change makers People who want to see change in the world and who make that change happen

cognitive Related to thinking and understanding

community A group of people who live, work, and play together

cultural Related to a particular group and its habits, beliefs, and traditions

depression A medical illness in which a person has repeated and severe feelings of sadness and hopelessness

disabilities Physical or mental conditions that limit a person's movements or activities

discrimination Treating a person or group differently from others

empathy Ability to understand feelings of others

ethnicity Belonging to a particular race

fail forward When design thinkers use their mistakes or failures to improve on their next try

gender The socially constructed characteristics of men and women. People can identify, or see themselves, as one or more genders.

inclusive Covering all the items or services required

mental illness Disorders that affect a person's mood, thinking, and behavior

mindset A set of attitudes held by someone

model A representation of something

Muslim A follower of the religion of Islam

observe (as in, observe religion) To celebrate

point of view (POV) question A question that defines the problem you will solve

point of view (POV) statement A statement that describes the user and his or her need

prejudice A feeling for someone that is not based on reason or logic

process A series of steps taken to achieve a particular goal

product An object that is made or modified

prototype The first model of something

race A group that shares the same history, language, and culture

Ramadan The ninth month of the Muslim year when people refrain from eating from sunrise to sunset

refugee A person who is forced to leave his or her home because of war, natural disaster, famine, or some other danger

respect To give someone or something admiration or attention

sexuality A person's sexual preference

storyboard A series of drawings that maps out a story, usually for making a video or cartoon

user The person or group with a problem that you are trying to solve

visual impairment A condition that impacts a person's ability to see

Index

About the Author

Janice Dyer has been working as a freelance editor and writer for over 20 years. She has written several nonfiction books for kids. She edits textbooks and other educational materials, nonfiction books, and reports.